Science, Maker, and Real Technology Students

S.M.A.R.T.S.

S.M.A.R.T.S. is published by Stone Arch Books
A Capstone Imprint
1710 Roe Crest Drive
North Mankato, MN 56003
www.capstonepub.com

Text and illustrations © 2016 Stone Arch Books

Library of Congress Cataloging-in-Publication Data is available on the
Library of Congress website.

ISBN: 978-1-4965-0463-0 (hardcover) 978-1-4965-0471-5 (paperback)
978-1-4965-2340-2 (eBook PDF)

Summary: When the centerpiece necklace from the local high school's Art
of Science show vanishes, everyone is stumped. There's no sign of a break-
in, and the door to the gallery was locked. Could the jewelry really just
disappear? It's up to the S.M.A.R.T.S. to solve the impossible crime.

Designer: Hilary Wacholz

For Matthew Radin, my science consultant

Printed in China by Nordica
0415/CA21500550
032015   008838NORDF15

S.M.A.R.T.S.

AND THE INVISIBLE ROBOT

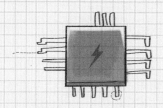

By Melinda Metz

Illustrated by Heath McKenzie

STONE ARCH BOOKS
a capstone imprint

1

"Okay, everyone, listen up! I have a surprise for you," Mrs. Ram — short for Mrs. Ramanujan — called to her students. All eleven kids in the makerspace — the community area at the back of the school's media center where students could meet to collaborate on ideas, robotics, science, and computers — turned toward her. Mrs. Ram patted the sheet covering the large table next to her. Something lumpy and bumpy was hidden underneath.

Jaden Thompson and Zoe Branson exchanged excited grins. There was nothing better than a surprise. The third member of their trio, Caleb Quinn, frowned.

"What's the problem?" Jaden asked him.

"People always think surprises are good," Caleb answered. "But what if you were Captain Marvel and found out you were an evil alien Skrull? Bad, bad surprise."

Zoe and Jaden laughed. Caleb was suspicious by nature. He always came up with the worst-case scenario for every situation.

"I doubt Mrs. Ram is going to tell us she just found out she's part of an alien invasion," Zoe replied. "Besides, I don't think an evil alien invader would be undercover as a fifth-grade teacher and S.M.A.R.T.S. sponsor."

S.M.A.R.T.S. — also known as Science, Maker, and Real Technology Students — was the name of the science club Hubble Middle School had started at the beginning of the school year. Zoe, Jaden, and Caleb had all joined right away.

"Exactly," Jaden agreed. "If you were an alien planning to take over the world, you'd want to be in a position of power. You'd want to be president, or a big celebrity, or the head of a massive company. Not a middle school teacher."

"You don't know . . ." Caleb began.

But before he could say anything else, Mrs. Ram held up both hands. "Quiet, please!" she called.

Everyone except Thing One and Thing Two — identical twins Benjamin and Samuel — instantly went silent. The twins kept arguing about what the surprise was going to be.

All the kids knew that when Mrs. Ram asked for quiet, she meant it. If kids didn't do what she said fast enough, she swore she'd give spoilers — big ones. And they knew she meant it. Mrs. Ram always went to the first showing of any movie with monsters or superheroes. She'd even go to a midnight show if there was one. And while she'd never actually told them anything that would ruin a movie, they all knew she could.

Sonja, the shortest girl in S.M.A.R.T.S., stood on her tiptoes, planted her hands on her hips, and glared at the twins. "The Ram said quiet!"

The twins immediately zipped their lips. Sonja was little, but she was fierce.

Mrs. Ram smiled. "Thank you, Sonja," she said. "We've been given a donation from the high school. They sent over a bunch of equipment they didn't use for a big exhibit they're doing combining art and science. Great, huh? Our club is barely a month old, and we already have so much cool stuff to experiment with!"

The group of students let out whoops of excitement.

"*Good* surprise, right?" Jaden asked Caleb.

"This time," Caleb admitted grudgingly.

Mr. Leavey, the school librarian, stepped out from behind his desk. "Are you ready to look?" he asked. As usual, his shirt was untucked and one of his shoes was untied. The kids often laughed that Mr. Leavey had trouble keeping himself as neat as he kept the media center.

"Yes!" everyone yelled, even Caleb.

Mr. Leavey whipped off the sheet covering the table. There was way too much to see at once — a ton of art supplies, miniature jumper cables, remote controls, sections of metallic track, a gear head, and tons of other stuff, even things like battery-operated toys and appliances. There was also a big bucket filled with ball bearings, bolts, springs, and other small parts.

"Awesome!" Zoe exclaimed. "Even *I* don't know what everything is."

"That thing on the end is a solar battery," Caleb told her. "My dad keeps one in the windshield of our car in case our regular car battery goes dead."

"With this donation, I think it's the perfect time for the club to explore robotics," Mrs. Ram said. "Can anyone give me an example of what we use robots for?"

"The Mars rovers are robots!" Zoe exclaimed, her brown eyes gleaming. She knew everything there was to know about the space program. Her dream was to become an astronaut and discover a new planet. She was still trying to come up with the perfect name. So far, her favorite was Oze, which was the letters of her name mixed up.

"Right!" Mrs. Ram said. "The rovers can take pictures of things as small as a strand of hair. They can take samples from deep in the ground. They can vaporize a rock and analyze what the rock is made of. We're learning so much from the information they're gathering."

"I don't think robots should have vaporizing capacity," Caleb muttered. "That's way too risky if you ask me."

Mrs. Ram started pacing back and forth. She always did that when she got excited, and she always got excited when she talked about science. "So what else do we use robotics for?"

"Surgery," Goo volunteered. Her name wasn't really Goo, but everyone in S.M.A.R.T.S. called her that because she came up with answers almost as fast as Google. She remembered almost everything she'd ever read!

"Definitely! A surgeon can control a robotic arm to use miniature instruments," Mrs. Ram answered. "Does anyone have an idea what industry uses the most robotics?"

"Car factories?" Jaden guessed.

Mrs. Ram's ponytail swished as she turned toward Jaden. "Bingo! Give that boy a prize! Robots are great for any job that's repetitive, dangerous, or requires precision." She grinned. "Now it's time to get your hands on our new stuff."

Jaden let out a whoop, and Zoe gave a happy bounce. Caleb scanned the table, already thinking about what he wanted to experiment with.

"Each of you take a few pieces of the equipment and brainstorm about how you could use them as robot parts," Mrs. Ram instructed. "Keep in mind there are four things every robot needs."

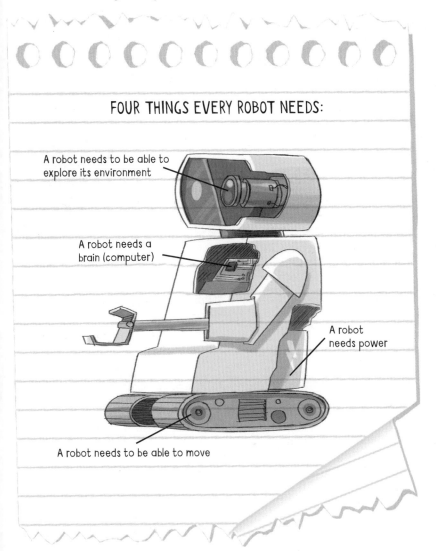

FOUR THINGS EVERY ROBOT NEEDS:

A robot needs to be able to explore its environment

A robot needs a brain (computer)

A robot needs power

A robot needs to be able to move

"Let your imaginations run wild!" Mrs. Ram exclaimed once she'd finished explaining the essential robot parts. "Ready, set —"

"Don't go," Mr. Leavey called. "Line up first. I don't want a disorganized charge toward the table." He tucked in his shirt but still didn't notice his shoe was untied.

Everyone started to line up behind Jaden. They knew he needed a little extra time. Jaden had cerebral palsy, CP, which made one of his legs and one of his arms really stiff and hard to move. He had to wear braces on his legs so he could walk.

"You guys want to team up and make something together?" Zoe suggested to Caleb and Jaden as they studied the equipment on the table. She picked up an electric toothbrush. "I'm taking this. The little motor could be a cool power source."

"I'm in," Jaden said, and Caleb nodded. They'd known each other since kindergarten but had never really hung out until they'd all joined S.M.A.R.T.S. That's when they'd discovered that they liked tons of the same stuff — science, of course, but also comics, video games, puzzles, and anything related to science fiction. Mrs. Ram did too!

At exactly the same time, Thing One and Thing Two both reached for something that looked like a round, flat Roomba vacuum cleaner, except bigger and with treads like a tank. Sometimes it was like the two of them shared one brain.

"Hey, Caleb, what's the name for a robot that doesn't want to destroy its maker?" Jaden asked as he picked up a set of plastic suction cups. He was already picturing using them to make their bot climb up a window!

Caleb didn't answer. He was studying a long piece of wire with a curved tip that was attached to a flat piece of plastic covered with little holes and small metal pins. "I wonder what this thing does."

"It's a touch sensor," Goo immediately answered.

Mrs. Ram came over to them. "When the wire touches something it sends a message to the microprocessor. The wire is like fingers for a robot, and the microprocessor is like the brain. You could program the robot to stop when the wire comes into contact with anything. That way the bot wouldn't crash into things." With that, she turned and headed over to Sonja, who was waving her arms to get the teacher's attention.

"Okay, back to my question, Caleb. Do you even remember what it was?" Jaden asked.

"A name for a robot that doesn't want to destroy its maker," Caleb repeated. His dark eyes were still locked on the touch sensor.

"Go on and tell us," Zoe urged. "But then you'll be down to one joke." She'd given Jaden a daily limit for his constant bad jokes, because she said too many of them in too short of a time would make her brain go *pop!*

"There isn't one," Jaden said. "Get it?"

Caleb's head jerked up. "You think there's something funny about a robot that destroys the person who built it? It could happen, Jaden. Then you wouldn't be laughing. You'd be DOOMED!"

"Maybe I should put a sound sensor on my robot. I'll program it so if I scream, the robot turns off," Zoe said.

"Unless the robot develops artificial intelligence," Caleb said, shoving his dark hair back off his forehead. "That means it would be able to think for itself. It wouldn't have to do what you told it to do anymore. And that would mean —"

"DOOM," Zoe and Jaden said together. They both knew it was Caleb's favorite word.

"That's right," Caleb answered. "Full-on DOOM."

The three of them stopped
courtyard with a statue
mascot, Champ the
long pole had
Champ

"Wow! Look at that!" Zoe exclaimed as she hurried down the covered walkway that connected the middle school to the high school. It was the day after S.M.A.R.T.S., and she, Caleb, and Mrs. Ram had decided to go over to the high school so they could thank the teacher who'd sent over all the equipment. Jaden couldn't come. He had physical therapy after school where he did stretches and exercises to keep his muscles as flexible as possible. It was a CP thing.

when they reached a

of the high school

Bulldog. Today a

been attached to one of

outstretched paws, and a

pe with a bucket at the end swung

back and forth from it. The bucket

spilled paint from a little hole

in the bottom onto a big piece

of poster board underneath.

The paint had made an

amazing design of

crisscrossing arcs.

Nearby, a girl stood watching the pattern that was

forming. "Hi!" she said, waving at the group. "Sorry I'm

kind of blocking the path. I'm using physics to make art."

"It's beautiful," Mrs. Ram replied.

"Thanks," the girl said with a proud smile. "It's for

the Art of Science exhibition. I'm using a pendulum to

paint."

"How does it work?" Caleb asked.

"It's super easy," the girl replied. "All I did was pull the bucket back and let it go to get it started."

"Ah," Mrs. Ram said. "The first Law of Motion in action. Once an object starts moving, it tends to stay moving."

"Exactly," the girl said with a smile. "The motion is making my painting. It's physics!"

"Awesome sauce on an ice cream sundae," Zoe said.

"Have you seen Ms. Jackson?" Mrs. Ram asked the girl. "She donated some really great robotics equipment to our science club — mostly stuff that didn't get used in the exhibition projects — and we wanted to thank her for it in person."

"She's probably over in the gallery," the girl replied. "We're displaying the projects all over school, but there are some that are too valuable or delicate to be left out. We have a room set up as a gallery for those. I'll take you."

"Thank you," Mrs. Ram said.

The girl smiled. "No problem. My boyfriend, Nathan, is over there anyway, and I want to say hi. I'm Taylor, by the way," she added. "Come on."

Zoe, Caleb, and Mrs. Ram followed Taylor into the main building and down the hall to an open door.

"Some people to see you, Ms. J.," Taylor called as she hurried over to a tall boy with red hair. He leaned close and whispered something in her ear that made her smile.

Mrs. Ram led the way around a large easel holding a display of metallic spider webs mounted on black paper. They looked incredibly realistic — almost like real webs that had somehow been coated with paint.

Ms. Jackson stood on the opposite side of the room wearing a paint-spattered smock. She wore deep red lipstick that matched the polish on her long, pointy nails.

"I brought over a couple of my students from the middle school science club," Mrs. Ram told the other teacher.

"We wanted to say thank you for everything you donated!" Zoe exclaimed.

"Even though some of it could be dangerous in the wrong hands," Caleb muttered.

"You're very welcome," Ms. Jackson answered. "We're just getting the last few pieces set up for our exhibit. These are three of our artists/scientists — Flora, Nathan, and Zac. And you've already met Taylor."

Nathan nodded in their direction and said hi, but the other two kids ignored them.

"Shouldn't you be working on your project, Taylor? It's the only one that isn't done, and the exhibition opens next Tuesday," Flora said. She examined the tall pedestal, which had several twists in its base, next to her.

Zoe noticed Flora was frowning, which seemed odd given that she was wearing a T-shirt and earrings covered with smiling frogs. She'd assumed someone who liked goofy frogs would be happier and more fun.

"No worries, Flora," Taylor answered. "It's working on itself right now." She winked at Caleb and Zoe.

"I'm glad you're here," Nathan said to Taylor. "I want to take a few pictures of you wearing the necklace." He walked over to the pedestal by Flora and picked up the necklace that lay on top. It was made of copper seashells and sparkly, light-blue gemstones.

Zoe noticed that the gems were almost the same color as Taylor's eyes. She gave a long sigh. "He has to be the best boyfriend ever," she whispered to Caleb. Caleb just snorted.

Nathan fastened the necklace around Taylor's neck, and Flora's frown turned into a scowl.

"I get how the pedestal combines science and art," Caleb said. "It's modeled after a DNA strand, right?" Sometimes he still had trouble wrapping his head around the fact that every single cell in his body was full of information that decided everything about him. The information was stored in genes, and genes were made of DNA. If he had different DNA, he'd be a different person!

Flora smiled for the first time. "You got it," she told Caleb. "It was a little hard to get the shape of the DNA just right — kind of like a ladder with twists in it. I made it out of a bunch of different kinds of paper layered together — scrapbook paper, origami paper, some regular printer paper. That made it flexible enough to bend around the curves without tearing. Then I painted over it."

Flora's scowl returned as Nathan began taking pictures of Taylor. Taylor giggled as she struck exaggerated supermodel poses.

"He didn't ask for your life story," the other boy, Zac, snapped. He didn't seem to like Flora very much. His nose wrinkled up when he looked at her, like he smelled something bad. Or maybe he just really hated frogs.

"How is the necklace connected to science?" Caleb asked. "Just because it's made out of shells?" He didn't think that was enough.

"No, I used chemistry to put the copper on the shells," Nathan answered. He put his cell phone away, and Taylor handed the necklace back to him. "I painted the shells with a solution that gave them a negative charge, then put them in a liquid that had positive copper ions in it. The positive ions were attracted to the negative charge of the shell's coating. After a couple hours, I had shells covered with copper."

"It's called electroforming," Mrs. Ram explained. "What about you, Zac? What did you make?"

"I made a pedestal too," Zac said. "Ms. J. gave us all different assignments, but one kid transferred, so now we have an extra pedestal and no necklace. Mine's not going to be used — hers is." He jerked his thumb at Flora. Her smile got as big as the ones on the frogs on the front of her T-shirt.

"It was a really hard choice," Ms. J. said. "I just thought Flora's pedestal was a better match with Nathan's necklace. And, Zac, you know your pedestal is still fantastic."

"But not good enough to be the main exhibit," Zac muttered, clearly still irritated about the teacher's decision.

Ms. Jackson ignored his comment. "Show them how yours works, Zac."

Zac walked over to a plastic column with an electronic keyboard and a bunch of colored light bulbs inside. He pressed a button, and the keys began to move. The column was filled with flashes of color as the bulbs flickered on and off in time with the music.

"It took a lot of tries, but I finally got the wiring and computer program right," Zac said. He gave his pedestal a pat. Then he looked over at Flora and frowned. "I think yours is a lot more art than science."

"I had to know about DNA to —" Flora started to say.

"Nope," Ms. Jackson interrupted. "We aren't having this conversation again. Everyone did a fabulous job. And that's it."

"Well, we should be getting back," Mrs. Ram said, changing the subject. "These two have to catch the late bus."

"And I need to lock up. That means everybody out," Ms. Jackson answered.

"Can't we stay just a little longer?" Flora begged.

Ms. Jackson shook her head. "Sorry. I have the only key, and I need to get home." She made a shooing motion, and everyone filed out of the room in front of her.

"Thanks again!" Zoe said once they were all out in the hall.

"Yeah, thanks," Caleb echoed.

"You're very welcome," Ms. Jackson replied as she locked the door behind her.

"That was so cool," Zoe said as they headed back to the middle school. "And you know what the best part was, Caleb?"

"What?" he asked.

"It's been another doom-free day," Zoe answered with a grin.

3

The next day, Zoe and Caleb headed back to the high school — this time with Jaden in tow. The three of them had agreed to meet up before school so Jaden could see some of the art-and-science combos.

"Hurry up," Jaden said. "If I'm going to get a chance to see what I missed yesterday, we have to get moving."

"I vote we stay outside and just look through the window of the gallery room," Zoe said as they walked. Classes hadn't started yet, and she didn't want to get in trouble for being inside when they weren't supposed to be.

"Good idea," Caleb agreed.

In the courtyard, Taylor's pendulum was still hanging from the bulldog statue. But unlike yesterday, it wasn't painting anything. Zoe led the way across the grass alongside the main school building.

"Hey! There's one we didn't see yesterday," Caleb said, pointing to a huge butterfly sculpture.

"It's amazing," Jaden said as he approached the piece. The butterfly had to be six feet tall. Its wings exploded with color.

"It says it's all made of trash," Zoe said, reading a sign next to the butterfly. "This tells how long it takes all parts to decompose." She was still studying the sign.

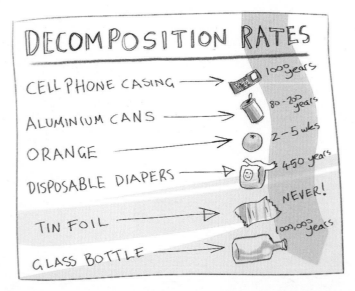

DECOMPOSITION RATES

CELL PHONE CASING ———> 1000 years

ALUMINIUM CANS ———> 80-200 years

ORANGE ———> 2-5 wks

DISPOSABLE DIAPERS ———> 450 years

TIN FOIL ———> NEVER!

GLASS BOTTLE ———> 1,000,000 years

"The plastic casing of a cell phone might take a thousand years to start breaking down in a landfill."

The three of them continued walking in silence, thinking about how long a thousand years was. When their great-great-great-great-great-great-great-great-great-great-great-great-great-great grandkids were born, the cell phone cases in the sculpture still might be around.

Finally, they reached the end of the building. "The gallery was the last room in the hallway, so this must be the window we need," Caleb said. He moved closer and peered into the room. "Oh, no!" he yelled.

Zoe pressed her face against the window so she could see into the gallery room. She tried to figure out what had gotten Caleb so upset. "What's the matter?" she asked. "Everything looks the same as it did yesterday."

"Except for one big difference!" Caleb exclaimed. "The pedestal is empty. Nathan's necklace is gone!"

4

"Hold up. There could be lots of reasons for why it's not there," Jaden said. He knew Caleb always thought everything was a disaster. "Nathan might have taken it out himself. Maybe he wanted to keep it in his locker for safekeeping."

Zoe shook her head. "The whole reason it was in the gallery was because Ms. Jackson wanted to keep everything that was valuable in a safe place. That's why she locked up behind us when we left. Why take it out?"

"He didn't — a thief did. Because it *is* valuable,"
Caleb answered. "And that's the reason people steal
stuff."

"Why do you think it's valuable?" Jaden asked. "The
way you guys described it, there was just a little layer
of copper over some shells. That wouldn't be worth
stealing."

"There were small gems in the necklace too. Light
blue ones. I'm pretty sure they were aquamarines," Zoe
added. "That's my birthstone. I don't know how much
they cost, though."

"I bet it's enough for someone to want to steal them."
Caleb shoved his fingers through his hair.

"Maybe we should find that teacher, Ms. Jackson,
and tell her," Jaden suggested.

"Yeah, she might know exactly where the necklace
is," Zoe agreed.

"Okay. Yeah. That's what we should do." Caleb
sucked in a deep breath. His mom was always telling
him to do that when he needed to calm down, and right

36

now definitely qualified as one of those times. "The sooner the search for the jewel thief starts, the better our are chances of catching him — or her."

"There's no evidence the necklace was stolen," Jaden reminded him. "Come on, we're science nerds. That means we should have all the facts before making a decision about something."

Caleb didn't reply. He just turned and started for the front doors. Zoe gave a shrug, then she and Jaden followed after him.

When they walked inside, they spotted Ms. Jackson right away. She was coming out of the main office with a stack of papers. Today her lips and long, sharp nails were painted berry pink.

"I didn't expect to see you two again so soon," Ms. Jackson said with a smile. "With, I'm assuming, another member of your club."

Jaden nodded.

Caleb got right to the point. "The necklace Nathan made has been stolen!" he burst out.

"We don't know that it's been stolen," Zoe corrected him. "But it's not on the pedestal."

"What do you mean?" Ms. Jackson exclaimed.

"We were outside and we looked in the window of the gallery. We wanted to show Jaden" — Zoe nodded toward him — "the projects we saw yesterday. And the necklace wasn't there."

"That can't be! I haven't unlocked the door since we all left yesterday afternoon," Ms. Jackson said. Her forehead wrinkled with worry. "I better go take a look."

Ms. Jackson didn't ask Zoe, Caleb, and Jaden to go with her, but they followed her anyway. No way were they going to miss what happened next.

"Do you think someone could have taken it yesterday before the door was locked?" Jaden asked.

Ms. Jackson glanced at him over her shoulder and shook her head. "I shooed everyone out in front of me. I remember looking at the pedestal before I walked away from it. The necklace was there."

They reached the door to the makeshift gallery, and Ms. Jackson fumbled to get the key in the lock. Finally there was a click, and the door opened. They all hurried around the spider-web display and over to the pedestal.

It was empty.

"You're right. It's gone!" Ms. Jackson cried.

"Maybe it just fell off," Zoe suggested hopefully.

"Yeah, right," Caleb muttered.

Zoe knelt down and scanned the carpet around the empty pedestal. "Nothing but a little carpet fuzz," she announced a moment later.

Jaden took a couple steps closer to the pedestal. His green eyes were serious as he studied it.

Zoe moved in for a closer look too. "Flora said she combined different kinds of paper so it would wrap around the twists of the DNA strand without ripping. But it cracked in a few places," she said as she traced a thin white line that circled the center of pedestal. There were several other white rings, some higher up, some lower.

She pointed to three scratches that ran across the top of the pedestal. They were almost thin enough to have been made by a cat's claw. "Were these little scratches on the top there yesterday?" Zoe asked.

"I'm not sure," Ms. Jackson answered, shaking her head.

"The necklace was covering most of the top at first," Caleb said. "I didn't look at the pedestal after Nathan took the necklace off and started taking pictures of Taylor wearing it. I'm sure Zoe didn't either. She was too busy wishing Nathan was her boyfriend." He made loud kissing noises.

"I was not!" Zoe exclaimed. "I just said he was a good boyfriend. Because he made Taylor a necklace with gems that matched her eyes."

"So *did* you see the scratches, Zoe?" Jaden asked her. His eyebrows had pulled together. That always happened when he was thinking hard.

Zoe shook her head. "They might have been there, but I don't remember."

Jaden's eyes kept flicking back and forth as he examined the top of the pedestal. "Do you think the necklace could have scratched the pedestal? Maybe the shells or the gemstones?"

"I don't think so," Caleb said. "There were probably fifteen stones on the necklace. It seems like if the aquamarines made the scratches there would be more of them."

"And the gems weren't that big. I think you'd have to really press down hard on one of them to make a scratch," Zoe added.

"I just don't understand," Ms. Jackson said before Jaden could ask more questions. "I know the windows were locked when I left yesterday. And Zoe and Caleb saw me lock the door."

"You're *sure* you saw the necklace after everyone else headed for the door?" Jaden asked.

"I'm positive," Ms. Jackson answered. "I remember because I was admiring how the necklace looked and thinking that I'd definitely made the right decision about which pedestal to use to display it. Zac did a great job, but the clear Plexiglas he used wouldn't have shown the necklace off as well as Flora's pedestal does."

"But that means the necklace disappeared from inside a locked room," Zoe said. "And that's impossible!"

5

"I absolutely remember seeing her lock the door yesterday," Mrs. Ram said later that afternoon. She and Jaden were sitting across from Zoe and Caleb at one of the tables in the media center's makerspace.

The three kids had asked her to meet them there after school, even though there wasn't a S.M.A.R.T.S. meeting. They wanted to find out what she remembered about the visit to the gallery in the hopes that it would help them figure out what had happened to the necklace.

Mrs. Ram had been shocked when they told her how the necklace had disappeared. She'd given them every detail she could remember from their time in the gallery, right up to Ms. Jackson locking the door after they all left the room.

"And you heard her say she had the only key, right?" Caleb asked.

Mrs. Ram nodded. "It's a true mystery."

"Jaden and I came in here during lunch and looked up the cost of aquamarines," Zoe told Mrs. Ram. "We wanted to see how valuable the ones in the necklace were."

"It depends on how big they are and how good they are, but we're guessing the ones Nathan used would be worth about a hundred and twenty dollars," Jaden explained.

"A hundred and twenty dollars," Caleb repeated. "And why do most people steal things, you guys? Money!"

"Well, it's a —" Mrs. Ram began.

But Caleb kept on talking. "All the thief has to do is take the gems out of the necklace and sell them. They could just do it online. It's brilliant. They wouldn't get caught. It's not like Nathan could identify the aquamarines from his necklace. The gems look like a million other ones."

"Bragging about how you stole my necklace?" someone demanded furiously.

The kids turned around and saw Nathan striding toward them — he didn't look happy. "One of you two took it," he said, looking from Zoe to Caleb. "I know it."

"You're accusing *us* of stealing it?" Caleb demanded.

"Yeah, I am," Nathan shot back.

"Enough," Mrs. Ram said quietly, but firmly. She turned in her chair so she could look at Nathan.

Nathan jerked his head down. He clearly hadn't realized there was a teacher at the table with them. Mrs. Ram was short and usually wore her hair in a ponytail, which made her look a lot like a kid from the back. A high school kid anyway.

"They were the last ones around the necklace before it was stolen," Nathan told her.

"If you want to talk to us, have a seat. And if everyone who was in the room yesterday afternoon is a suspect, that includes me," Mrs. Ram told Nathan.

"I know you didn't do it," Nathan muttered, still standing. "And Flora and Zac wouldn't do it. They're my friends. Taylor knew I was going to give her the necklace, so there's no reason for her to take it. And for sure Ms. Jackson wouldn't."

Mrs. Ram didn't say anything. She just pointed to a chair and waited until Nathan sat down. Once he was seated, she calmly said, "You don't know what happened to the necklace."

"This morning those two" — he pointed from Zoe to Caleb — "were sneaking around the school. Everyone knows criminals like to return to the scene of the crime. They want to see how upset everyone is."

"I was with them this morning," Jaden said quickly. "We were there because they wanted me to see the cool stuff you and your friends made for the show. We weren't sneaking."

"And as soon as we noticed that the necklace was gone, we went right to Ms. Jackson," Zoe explained. "We were the ones that told her about it."

"Which is *exactly* what smart thieves would do," Nathan snapped. "They'd pretend to be worried about the necklace. That way no one would suspect them!" By the time he finished speaking, Nathan was so mad his face was almost as red as his hair.

Caleb's face was getting red too. "We wouldn't —"

But Nathan wouldn't let him get a word in. "You're all in the science club," he interrupted. "That means you're smart. You'd have a plan to make sure no one would blame you."

"Nathan," Mrs. Ram said firmly, "I understand why you're upset. You worked hard on that necklace."

"I did. And I made it for Taylor. She was so excited when I first showed it to her. She loved it," Nathan said, his voice getting softer.

"I'm sure she did. But no matter how upset you are, it isn't okay to accuse these kids of stealing. You have no proof. That's right, isn't it?" Mrs. Ram asked.

Nathan hesitated but finally nodded.

"Then I think you should go now, Nathan," Mrs. Ram said, sounding sterner than the kids could ever remember.

Nathan stood up and headed for the door. But he stopped for a second when he was behind Mrs. Ram. That way she didn't see him when he glared at Caleb and Zoe and mouthed the words, "I know you did it."

6

A few hours later, the kids were still in the media center. They hadn't felt like going home right away after Nathan's big blow up. Instead they'd gotten permission from their parents to take the late bus and were using the extra time to help Mr. Leavey shelve books. He deserved it after all the work he'd done helping with the makerspace.

"Between the three of us, I'm sure we can figure out who stole the necklace," Zoe said. "I know it. Jaden's read every Sherlock Holmes story ever written. He practically has them memorized. And we're all science geeks. We know how to make careful observations and think about them logically."

"I'm in. I've always wanted to say 'the game is afoot,'" Jaden said from where he sat on a chair between two rows of shelves. Zoe and Caleb stood on either side of him. "That's Sherlock for 'yo, I've got a criminal to catch.'"

"I don't care if Nathan gets his necklace back or not," Caleb muttered. "He's been a total jerk to all of us." He handed Jaden a book that he could put on the shelf from the chair he sat in. Sometimes Jaden got wobbly if he stood still for a long time. It was a CP thing, at least for him.

"Yeah, a jerk on toast," Zoe agreed, sliding a book into place. "But he was upset, because it was something special he made for Taylor. And besides, it's not just about getting the necklace back. It's about proving we didn't steal it!"

"Ugh! Why didn't I think of that?" Caleb burst out. "Nathan could be at the police station right now telling everyone I'm a thief. I could end up in jail. It's arrived. I knew it would. DOOM!"

"Caleb, chill. You're in fifth grade. Fifth graders don't go to jail. And besides, you know Mrs. Ram doesn't think you did it," Jaden reminded him. "You or Zoe."

"That's because Mrs. Ram knows us," Caleb protested.

"What if Nathan goes around telling everyone we did it?" Zoe said. "My big sister, Kylie, is in high school with him! It would be so embarrassing for her to have people saying her little sister is a thief!" She was starting to sound almost as worried and upset as Caleb had moments earlier. "I don't want anyone thinking I would steal something."

"The first thing we should do is make a list of suspects," Jaden told them. "Sherlock would probably start with the last people who saw the necklace before it was stolen." He struggled to put a book on a shelf above his head but managed to slide it into place on the second try.

"That means the suspect list is me, Zoe, Taylor, Nathan, Flora, Ms. Jackson, and Mrs. Ram," Caleb told him.

"Mrs. Ram didn't do it. Or you," Zoe told Caleb firmly. "Or me!" She stood on tiptoe to put a book on the top shelf.

"The list is just a starting place," Jaden said. "Now we need to think about motive. Why would someone steal the necklace?"

"We already know why — money," Caleb said.

"Money is one possibility," Jaden agreed. "But could there be any other reasons?"

SUSPECTS

MISSING!

FLORA

TAYLOR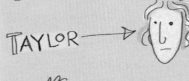

 NATHAN

Ms. JACKSON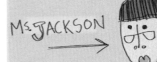

 Mrs. RAM

MOTIVES

MONEY

Zoe thought for a few moments, then said, "Zac was mad that Flora's pedestal was going to be used to hold the necklace instead of his. He said he didn't think her project had enough science in it. And you should have seen Zac's face when he looked at Flora. It was like he was about to puke." She grinned. "Guess I get to be Watson."

"I don't think so," Caleb told her. "I said money before you said the thing about Zac. And our Sherlock said that was a good motive."

"Maybe we're less like Holmes and Watson and more like the Avengers — a team," Jaden suggested.

"I call Iron Man!" Caleb announced.

Zoe rolled her eyes. "Maybe I want to be Iron Man," she said. "Or maybe Jaden does." She looked over at Jaden, and her expression grew serious. "How incredible would that be? The suit could wrap around you, and you'd be able to do anything."

"Your arm and legs would be stronger than strong. They'd be superhero strong," Caleb added. "Hey, I have an idea! We don't have the Iron Man suit, but maybe we could make you something with all the new robotics equipment."

Zoe suddenly wondered if it bothered Jaden that they were talking about his body like it was something that needed to be fixed. He only ever asked for help when there was something he absolutely couldn't do for himself. The rest of the time, he handled things alone, no matter how hard it was.

"Is it . . . okay? That we're talking about you like . . ." Zoe couldn't finish the sentence. She didn't know how.

"I didn't mean that you'd be better if you were part robot," Caleb said quickly. "You already do everything you need to do."

Jaden grinned at his friends. "Yeah, but that doesn't mean we couldn't come up with some invention that would make me even more awesome," he said.

"You're not mad?" Zoe asked. She thought she'd be mad if people started talking about ways they could improve her.

"Not mad," Jaden answered, shaking his head. He actually thought it was pretty cool that his friends wanted to come up with robotics inventions to help him. "Hey, what do you call it when a dinosaur crashes his car?"

Zoe smiled. It was all good if Jaden was starting one of his goofy jokes.

Caleb sighed. "What?" he asked.

"Tyrannosaurus wrecks." Jaden put the book he was holding on the shelf and cracked up. "Get it? Tyrannosaurus rex, Tyrannosaurus wrecks?"

"We get it," Zoe told him. "You just didn't hear us laughing because that might offically be your dumbest joke ever."

"Do you think there's something we could invent to stop all the bad jokes from coming out of your mouth?" Caleb wondered aloud, studying Jaden. "Maybe some kind of face mask with a little door that could slide over your mouth if it picked up on any stupid-joke brain waves."

Zoe smiled. "I think that might be pushing it, but at least now we have a good use for all those donated robotics supplies. We'll come up with an amazing invention for Jaden!"

7

The next afternoon, the kids were back in the
makerspace. Each table had a group of S.M.A.R.T.S. kids
working on building robots with the new equipment.

"I have a great idea for what to make for Jaden,"
Caleb announced. He'd been thinking a lot about how
Jaden hadn't been able to put books away on the top
shelves yesterday. "A robotic arm with an extender. That
way you'd be able to reach whatever you wanted, even
when you're sitting down."

"Then I could always grab the last piece of cake. Even if it's sitting right in front of my brother!" Jaden exclaimed. "That'd be awesome."

"Oooh. We should figure out a way to make it invisible, like with some kind of special coating," Zoe jumped in. "Then if your brother got mad, you could just tell him it's not your fault the cake floated over to your plate."

Jaden laughed. "That's brilliant! And each finger should be able to do something different. One could be a cryptographic sequencer — that's the thing Batman has on his utility belt that can hack into any computer. And one could be a skeleton key, so I could get into any room."

"Love it!" Zoe agreed. "I'd use it to open my sister's diary. I know Kylie writes stuff about me in there, and if it's about me, I should be able to read it."

"I think one finger needs to be a metal detector," Caleb added. "Think how much spare change you could find!"

"One could have a tiny camera. One could make a whistling sound that calls dogs. Or birds!" Zoe exclaimed. "Summoning a flock of birds would be *so* cool. If you got enough of them, they could pick you up and fly you places."

Both boys stared at her like she was nuts.

"What?" Zoe said. "It could work. It would take a lot of birds, but it could."

"Maybe . . ." Caleb said slowly. "But I think one of the fingers should be able to release a parachute if you're going to trust a bunch of birds to fly you around. At least then you'd have a backup plan."

Mrs. Ram dropped down in the empty seat at their table. "How's it going? Did you decide what you want to make yet?"

"A robotic arm," Jaden said. "One that can stretch out really far with a hand that can grab things. We want it to do a bunch of other stuff too, but that's the first thing." He looked over at Caleb and Zoe, and they nodded.

"That's a good choice," Mrs. Ram said. "A lot of robotics are actually based on parts of the human body. Like where we use eyes to see, a robot uses a camera. It might help you design a robotic arm if you think about how your own arm works."

Mrs. Ram turned to face the rest of the S.M.A.R.T.S. kids. "Anyone know what makes a human arm bend and straighten?" she called out.

"Muscles," Goo immediately answered.

"Right!" Jaden exclaimed. "My physical therapist talked to me about it. There are muscles covering our skeletons. There are triceps muscles in your arms. When you tighten them, they pull on your elbow, which makes it straighten, and your arm extends. If you tighten your bicep muscles, your elbow bends, and your arm goes the other way."

"So we need to come up with the robot version of muscles and bones," Zoe said.

"Rubber bands might work for muscles, because —" Thing One, Benjamin, began.

BOT

HUMAN

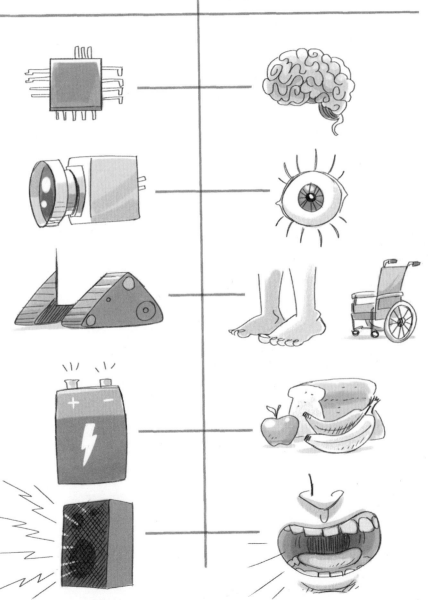

"— they're stretchy," Thing Two, Samuel, finished. The twins finished each other's sentences a lot.

"Very clever, boys," Mrs. Ram said. "For bones, I think there are some pieces of metal with the donations from the high school. They already have some holes cut in them, which would make it easier to create a joint. Since the arm has to be able to bend if you want it to extend, you'll need one. There are some grippers in there too. Call me if you need help." With that, Mrs. Ram stood up and headed to the next table.

"I'll get the stuff," Caleb said, but he didn't get up right away.

"What?" Zoe asked.

"I just can't stop thinking about the necklace," Caleb said. "What if we really end up in jail? What if Nathan tells his parents that we stole his necklace, and they tell the police, and —"

Jaden interrupted him before he got too agitated. "There's no way you're going to jail. You're not even going to the principal's office. You need to relax."

"Nobody's even going to be able to spread rumors that one of us took the necklace," Zoe told Caleb. "Because we're going to catch the thief. Now go get the stuff."

Caleb got up and headed for the big table loaded with all the supplies left over from the Art of Science projects.

"Maybe we should try to figure out some other possible motives while we work on the arm," Jaden said quietly. "We've got to solve the case fast, or Caleb is going to lose it."

"Maybe it would help if we focused on the *how* instead of the *why*," Zoe suggested. "Someone came up with a way to get that necklace out of a locked room. If we can figure it out too, maybe that will give us some clues."

Caleb came back and dumped a bunch of metal strips on the table in front of them. "I got a little motor too. We need to have some way to make the rubber bands get tighter."

"Maybe we could make the motor turn a little spool!" Zoe exclaimed. "The bands would get tighter and tighter the more times they wrapped around the spool. And if the spool turned in the opposite direction, they'd get looser."

"What else did you get?" Jaden asked curiously, peering at the supplies.

"I found a gripper that's already shaped like a hand," Caleb said, placing it in the middle of the table so Jaden and Zoe could see it.

Jaden bent and straightened a few of the shiny fingers. "Nice. It feels really strong too. It should be able to pick up something pretty heavy."

"With an extender, I bet you could use the hand to do things like put a book on a high shelf," Zoe said.

Sonja looked over from the next table. "I want one. I'm always having to ask people to reach things for me," she said.

"Once we figure out how to make one for Jaden, maybe we'll make a bunch and sell them," Caleb said. "We need a cool name. The Snaker?"

Zoe shook her head. "I don't think so. Not everyone likes snakes," she said. "I think we should name it after Jaden."

"Well, my name *is* cooler than anything else," Jaden joked.

"We'll put you down for the first Jaden arm, right after Jaden," Caleb told Sonja.

"That's it! Jaden. Arm. JadArm!" Zoe exclaimed. She high-fived both boys.

The JadArm

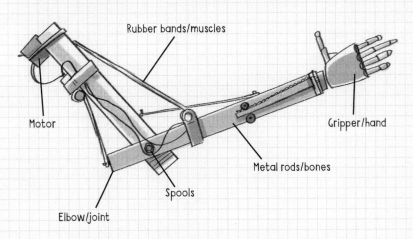

Rubber bands/muscles

Motor

Gripper/hand

Metal rods/bones

Spools

Elbow/joint

"How long do you think the extender should be?" Caleb asked Jaden. He'd be the one using it, so it should be his call. "What's the highest thing you need to reach?"

"The extender doesn't have to only go up. It could go straight out too," Jaden said.

"Yeah, but you wouldn't need it to, right?" Zoe asked.

"*I* wouldn't," Jaden answered. "I could just walk over to whatever I wanted to get if it was in reach. But what if I couldn't?"

"If you couldn't walk, wouldn't you have a wheelchair?" Caleb said.

"Yeah, but that wouldn't help if what I wanted to get to was on the other side of a locked door," Jaden said. He looked from Zoe to Caleb. He could see the moment Caleb got it.

Caleb straightened, and a smile broke across his face. "Like if you were a jewel thief and needed to get to a necklace that was in a locked room. Genius!"

"The arm could go under the door and then stretch out," Zoe agreed.

"We have a hypothesis," Jaden said. "Now we have to get the extender part of the arm working so we can test it."

Caleb gave a fist pump. "Then tomorrow we can take it over to the high school and see what the JadArm can do!"

8

"There's somebody snooping around at the crime scene!" Caleb exclaimed as they walked into the high school before class the next morning. He stared down the hallway at the gallery room.

Zoe nudged him out of the way so she could see for herself. "It's Zac! And he's on our suspect list!"

"Right. Motive: he wanted his pedestal to be used to display the necklace, not Flora's," Jaden said. "Without the necklace, neither pedestal will have anything on it."

"Cover me!" Caleb ordered. Then he took off down the hall toward Zac.

"Cover him?" Jaden said. "What is he going to do?"

"I have no idea," Zoe answered.

"Go," Jaden urged. "I'll be behind you. Don't let him do anything stupid."

"I think it's already too late," Zoe muttered as she took off after Caleb.

"I go to school here!" Zac shouted as Zoe ran down the hall. "What are *you* doing here?"

"I'm the one asking the questions!" Caleb yelled.

Zoe skidded to a stop next to them. "Hey! Hi! What's up?" She gave Zac a big smile.

"He won't tell me why he's down here," Caleb snapped. He moved closer to Zac, getting in his face. Or at least getting sort of close to his face. Zac was about a foot taller than Caleb. "Are you planning to steal something else?"

Zoe grabbed Caleb by the hood of his sweatshirt and pulled him back a few steps. "Sorry, Zac. He's freaking out a little because Nathan came over to our school the other day and accused *us* of stealing the necklace."

"Ask him what he's doing down here, sneaking around," Caleb demanded.

"He doesn't have to —" Jaden began as he reached them.

"It's fine," Zac interrupted. "I was actually down here trying to figure out how someone could have gotten the necklace out of the room with the door locked."

"Yeah, right," Caleb said.

"Whatever, I don't need this," Zac muttered. He strode off without looking back.

Caleb twisted away from Zoe. "That's not what I meant when I said 'cover me,'" he snapped.

"Let's just do what we came here to do," Zoe said. "For all we know, Zac went to get Ms. Jackson. Or the principal."

Caleb took the newly assembled JadArm out of his backpack and knelt down in front of the door. Zoe and Jaden stood over to his left side so they could see

through the small window in the door of the makeshift gallery.

Their theory was that the thief had used an arm like the one they'd made to get the necklace out. Now it was time to see if they were right.

They went to slide the arm under the door, and ran into problem number one — it didn't fit.

"The JadArm hand is thinner than a human one, but it's still too big to fit under the door," Caleb said.

"That's not the only problem," Jaden said. "We forgot about the spider-web display. It's between the door and the pedestal. Even if we could make the JadArm thinner and longer, we wouldn't be able to wrap it around the web display. I should have made a sketch of the crime scene as soon as we got back to school the other day."

As they started back down the hall, Caleb's shoulders were slumped and his head drooped. All the anger seemed to have drained out of him.

"Don't worry, coming over here wasn't a total bust," Jaden said. "At least we can eliminate one suspect."

"Who?" Zoe asked, confused. "Please explain to your Watsons."

"Zac said he was over here trying to figure out how someone got the necklace out of the room when it was locked," Jaden explained. "He wouldn't be doing that if he was the one who took it."

"But he was lying!" Caleb protested.

Jaden shook his head. "I don't think so. If he took the necklace, why would he be hanging around the gallery room? If he's the thief, he already has what he wants — the necklace. And he already knows how he got it out."

"That makes sense," Zoe admitted as they headed back outside. "We're making progress. Progress, I tell you. So smile, Caleb."

"I'm still not sure that guy Zac can be trusted," Caleb grumbled. "But I guess what you said makes sense."

Jaden suddenly stopped walking. "Uh-oh."

"What?" Caleb exclaimed. "Uh-oh what?"

"Nathan's over there by the bulldog statue with some girl," Jaden explained.

"That's Taylor," Zoe told him. "She's his girlfriend, the one he made the necklace for. We have to go by him to get back to our school. Let's just hope he's calmed down by now."

"I haven't calmed down," Caleb announced.

"Calm down *now*, then," Jaden told him.

The three of them started walking again, but they'd only taken a few steps when someone behind them yelled, "I know you! The science club kids from the middle school."

Zoe looked over her shoulder and saw Flora trotting toward them.

"That's us," Zoe said. "This is our friend Jaden. He couldn't make it the other day. Cute shoes," she added, nodding at Flora's sneakers, which were covered with dancing frogs.

"Thanks!" Flora answered. "I just got them at the mall last night. I got a present for Nathan too. Look!" She

81

pulled a small box out of her purse and opened it. A pearl bracelet lay inside.

"That's for *Nathan*?" Caleb asked.

Flora laughed. "It's so he can make a new necklace. He can take apart the bracelet and use the pearls," she explained, her voice filled with excitement. "I love pearls almost as much as frogs. Nathan already made some new copper-covered shells. I think the pearls will look better with them than those aquamarines did. I can't wait to show him! I'll see you around!" With that she took off, calling out Nathan's name.

"New shoes *and* a bracelet," Jaden said. "Wonder how much she spent on her shopping trip?"

Caleb's eyes widened. "Are you thinking it might be about as much she'd get from selling some aquamarines?"

"But what would her motive be?" Zoe asked. "She was really happy her pedestal was going to have the necklace on it."

"The motive is what I always said it was — money." Caleb pulled out his cell and used it to do a quick web search. "It looks like you could get a bracelet like the one Flora had for less than thirty bucks. We said the aquamarines were worth about a hundred and twenty dollars. If she sold them, she could have bought Nathan the pearls for his necklace *and* had plenty left over for herself."

"Like for new shoes," Zoe said.

"*And* she'd still get to have one of Nathan's necklaces on her podium in the exhibition," Jaden said. "Giving him the pearls makes sure of that."

"My sister knows tons of people at the high school," Zoe said. "I'll text her and ask what she knows about Flora, otherwise known as our new number-one suspect."

9

"Could you fart for me?" Caleb asked as soon as Zoe flopped down in her usual chair in the makerspace that afternoon. Mrs. Ram was letting them have extra S.M.A.R.T.S. sessions because everyone in the group was so eager to keep working on their bots.

"What? No!" Zoe stared at him like he'd suddenly grown two heads. "Why?"

"I want to record some fart noises and see if I can make a robotic fart-detector," Caleb said. "Every time my cousin sleeps over, he says I fart in my sleep. I want to prove that *he's* the one doing it. The robot could point in the direction the stink came from."

Zoe sighed. They were still going to do more work on the JadArm, but they'd decided to play around with some other robotics projects too. And that's what Caleb had come up with — a fart-detector. Boys.

"Goo, what makes a fart smelly?" Jaden called over to her.

"Sulfur," Goo answered without even looking up from her project — attaching spider legs to a battery-operated car.

"Thanks," Jaden called, then he turned back to Caleb. "There should be a way for a robot to sense sulfur in the air. We have a carbon monoxide monitor in our house. Maybe it could work like that."

Caleb nodded. "I need to talk to Mrs. Ram." He looked around the room and spotted her standing a couple tables away. She was punching buttons on her cell phone and laughing.

"Hey, no phones in the media center, Mrs. Ram!" Caleb joked.

"It's not a phone," Mrs. Ram replied. "It's a remote control." She pointed to the ground where the thing that looked like an extra-large Roomba with treads was chugging toward them. It made a right turn, then a left turn, then another right.

"Benjamin and Samuel found a program we could download to my phone," Mrs. Ram explained. "It's letting me control the bot with my phone."

"Coolness!" Zoe exclaimed.

"Next we're going to attach some markers to it and then —" Thing One began.

"— it will be an Artbot, and we can use it to draw pictures!" his brother finished for him.

"We're so going to be ready when we get to high school and have an Art of Science exhibition," Jaden said.

"Well, when you're done, I need to ask you a question," Caleb called over to Mrs. Ram.

"I'll be over in a minute," she promised.

"Hey, Caleb, what kind of teacher passes gas?" Jaden asked.

"What kind?" Caleb asked. Zoe pressed her fingers into her ears to block the joke.

"A tutor. Get it? Toot!" Jaden laughed, the way he always laughed at his dumb jokes.

"I still heard that," Zoe said, pulling her fingers away from her ears. "We really are going to have to make that bad-joke stopper. Jaden needs it right now!"

"I thought that one was pretty funny," Caleb answered.

"Of course you did," Zoe said, rolling her eyes. She pulled a roll of paper out of a big shopping bag and spread the paper out on one end of the table.

"What's that for?" Jaden asked.

"I want to try to make a pair of wings that really flap," she said. "I made the paper the way Flora said she did, because I needed it to be flexible. Then I painted it so it looked like peacock feathers!"

"What do you want the wings for?" Caleb asked. He picked up their robotic arm and made it extend.

"I get to have a Halloween party this year, and I want a fab costume. You're invited, so you have to come up with costumes too," Zoe told them. "I thought I could make the wings kind of like a paper fan. You know how you can flick them open? I was hoping I could come up

with a robotic way to flick my wings open and pull them closed."

"Maybe you could use an umbrella as a model," Jaden suggested. "You know how you just push a button and the umbrella pops open? There should be a way to do that using robotics. Maybe even with a remote."

"A remote! That would be amazing. I could wave them all night long!" Zoe exclaimed. "I need to take apart an umbrella to see how it works."

"Already did it last year," Caleb announced. "Already got yelled at for doing it. I keep telling my parents that taking stuff apart is educational, but they don't seem to get it. That's the best way to learn how something works!"

Jaden and Zoe laughed. Caleb was always taking stuff apart. The problem was, he didn't always remember to put it back together.

"An umbrella's pretty basic," Caleb continued. "The handle has a little ring that slides up and down it, and there are metal spokes attached to it. When the ring is

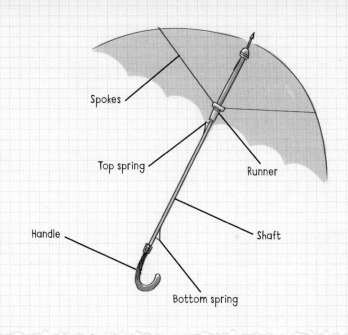

Spokes

Top spring

Runner

Handle

Shaft

Bottom spring

at the bottom, it pulls the spokes flat against the handle. When the ring is at the top, it pushes the spokes up and out."

Caleb sucked in a deep breath. "With some umbrellas you push the ring up with your fingers. But like Jaden said, with some you can push a little button. That lets a spring inside the handle power the ring to the top."

"Great description, Caleb," Mrs. Ram said as she walked over. "Now, what did you need help with?"

Before Mrs. Ram could answer, Zoe's cell vibrated. She knew phones were supposed to be turned off in the media center, but she also knew she was trying to solve the case of the stolen the necklace.

"Be right back," Zoe said, hurrying to the bathroom. She flipped open her phone and saw a text from her sister.

Hi, Z. Flora has $$$ to spare. New clothes, new shoes, new everything all the time. No b-friend. Super smart. Friendly. Hearts frogs. And pearls. Enuff?

Zoe texted back a thanks, then hurried back to her table.

"I just got some great ideas for my fart detector from The Ram," Caleb said as she sat down.

Zoe shook her head. "Do we have to talk about farts? Or can we talk about how the girl who was our top suspect this morning isn't a suspect anymore?"

"What?" Caleb demanded.

"Kylie texted me back with info about Flora," Zoe explained, giving them the rundown on what her sister had said. "She said Flora buys new stuff all the time. She wouldn't have needed to steal the aquamarines to get cash for a trip to the mall."

Jaden sighed. "So we don't have a motive for Flora anymore," he said.

"Exactly," Zoe answered.

Caleb groaned. "We already said we don't think Zac's the thief. And now we don't think Flora is either. Who are we left with?"

"Well, there's Taylor — but I don't know why she would steal the necklace. She knew Nathan was going to give it to her as soon as the exhibition was over," Zoe added.

Jaden nodded. "And Nathan wouldn't have stolen his own necklace. It would make no sense. We all saw how mad he was after it vanished."

"So that just leaves . . ." Zoe hesitated, then went on, "Caleb, me, Mrs. Ram, and Ms. Jackson."

"Unless we're missing something, it's down to those four," Jaden said.

Jaden's stomach clenched itself into a tight ball. "I don't know what we should do next," he admitted.

"What would Sherlock do?" Caleb asked.

"Review the evidence," Jaden said. "We keep going over the suspects and getting nowhere. We need another approach. What else do we have?"

"Locked doors, locked windows, aquamarines worth a hundred and twenty bucks, scratches on the pedestal, one set of keys —" Caleb began.

Zoe's eyes lit up. "Scratches! Scratches!" she hollered.

"Yeah, I said that," Caleb told her. "We need —"

"Do you guys remember Ms. Jackson's nails?" Zoe interrupted.

"Um, no," Caleb and Jaden said.

"Boys." Zoe shook her head. They never noticed the important things. "Her nails were really long — and pointy."

"Sherlock definitely would have caught that," Jaden told her. "Pointy nails could make thin scratches. If she grabbed the necklace, her nails could have scraped the top of the pedestal. That means Ms. Jackson is now our top suspect. She wouldn't have had to get through a locked door either. She has the key."

"But why would she take one of her students' art projects?" Caleb asked.

"I guess that's the next thing we need to figure out," Jaden answered.

10

Monday morning, Zoe got to school early and waited
for Jaden and Caleb by their row of lockers. She had
news. Not good news, but important news.

A few moments later, the boys walked down the
hall together. Zoe raced over to them. "Ms. Jackson's
fingernails didn't make the scratches on the pedestal,"
she announced.

"What?" Caleb burst out. "How do you know?"

"I got Kylie to take me to the drug store, and I
bought packages of all the longest, pointiest fake nails I

could find," Zoe explained. "I know some of them were even pointier than Ms. Jackson's. I'd been working on my wings at home, and I figured it would be the perfect way to test our theory. I used about the same mix of paper that Flora said she used for her pedestal, and I think the same kind of paint."

Zoe pulled one wing out of a big shopping bag. The wing was folded up like an accordion. She opened it up part way. The paint had cracked, and thin white lines ran down every place where she'd folded it.

"Look," she said, pointing to a bunch of little scratches along one edge. "I made those with the nails."

Jaden studied them. "You're right. They don't seem to match the ones on the pedestal. These scratches are all way thicker," he agreed.

"I know! I thought for a second I'd solved the case, but it was a total fail!" Zoe said with a frown.

"That means we have to cross her off the suspect list," Caleb said. "This is hopeless! It's down to Mrs. Ram, Zoe, and me now. We know we didn't do it — but there's no one left!"

"Maybe we need to go back to the high school one more time," Jaden suggested. "There could be a clue we missed in the gallery room."

* * *

As soon as the last bell rang, Jaden, Caleb, and Zoe met up and headed for the high school. "I've got a joke for you," Jaden said as they walked. "Sherlock Holmes and Watson go camping —"

"Okay, but this is your last bad joke of the day," Zoe warned him. She only allowed him three a day, and he'd already used up two.

Jaden kept going. "They lay in a clearing looking up at the sky. 'Tell me what you observe,' Sherlock says to Watson. And Watson says, 'I see stars. Most look like single specks of light, but in fact, the majority are binary pairs — two stars orbiting around each other. I see the moon. It is the fifth largest moon in our solar system.'"

Jaden looked over at Zoe and Caleb to make sure they were paying attention, then continued. "'Watson, you'll never be a detective!' Holmes exclaims. 'Your first observation should have been that our tent has been stolen, which is why we can see the sky at all.'"

Zoe giggled. "That doesn't count as a bad joke. I liked it. So you still have one stinker left for the day."

"Who took the tent?" Caleb asked.

Jaden shook his head. "I don't know. It's just a joke."

"It's just wrong not to say who took it." Caleb shoved his fingers though his hair. Almost every strand was sticking up now. Even in a joke, an unsolved mystery bothered Caleb.

"Look. The door to the gallery is open," Zoe said when they reached the long hallway that led to the room. "I wonder if Nathan's in there."

"Doesn't matter if he is," Jaden said. "We haven't done anything wrong." But his heart started beating a little faster when they reached the room.

Inside, Flora was kneeling by her pedestal, doing some touch-ups with a small paintbrush. The frog pendant she wore swung back and forth on its chain of little pearls when she stood up. "Back again?" she asked.

"It's just so cool seeing all the projects," Zoe said. She didn't want to admit that they were there to solve a mystery. "Nice necklace," she added.

"Thanks, it's new," Flora said with a smile. "I love frogs and I love pearls, so when I saw it, I knew I had to have it."

"Hi, Flora," Taylor said as she came into the room and walked over to them. The smile quickly disappeared from Flora's face.

"Hi, fellow science geeks," Taylor added to Zoe, Caleb, and Jaden.

Everybody said hi back except Flora. She knelt back down by the pedestal and started painting again.

"Have you seen Nathan?" Taylor asked.

Zoe shook her head. "Was he supposed to meet you here?" she asked.

Taylor nodded. "Mmm-hmm. We told Ms. Jackson we'd help get the room ready. And he has to bring over his new necklace. He finished it last night. His parents even bought him some more aquamarines."

"What? But he had the pearls I bought him!" Flora exclaimed.

Taylor shrugged. "He said he wanted it to be exactly the same, because he knew how much I loved the first one," she answered.

"That's so great!" Zoe told her.

Jaden moved a little closer to Flora. "Why are you repainting it? The pedestal looks awesome."

Zoe peered over his shoulder. Flora was using the brush to paint over the thin white lines that circled the pedestal's base in several places.

She'd already repainted the thin scratches that had been on top.

"I don't think anyone would notice those cracks in the paint," Zoe said. "They're not very big."

Flora flushed. "I just want it to be perfect," she answered. "The exhibit starts tomorrow. I don't think the paint will crack again before that."

Jaden opened his mouth, but before he could say anything, an angry shout drew everyone's attention. "Get out!" someone yelled.

Caleb, Jaden, and Zoe all recognized the angry voice right away — Nathan. They turned around and saw him standing in the doorway.

"I have my new necklace, and I don't want you three in the same room with it," Nathan yelled as he rushed toward them.

"Nathan, calm down," Taylor said.

"He has the right to be upset," Flora jumped in. "They were in here right before the necklace disappeared. Who else could have taken it?"

Zoe and the boys exchanged confused looks. Flora had been friendly and welcoming when they'd first arrived, but now she sounded almost as angry with them as Nathan did.

"Out!" Nathan repeated.

"Okay," Jaden said. "We'll go. But the necklace was stolen after everyone left the room."

"But Ms. Jackson locked the door," Flora reminded him.

"I know," Jaden replied. "I also know exactly how it was stolen."

Caleb and Zoe both turned to look at Jaden in surprise. What was he talking about?

"Of course you know how it was stolen," Nathan shot back. "One of your friends took it, and they told you."

"Yeah," Flora agreed. "How else could you know?"

"I just figured it out," Jaden answered. "And the leftover equipment Ms. Jackson donated will help me prove it."

Caleb and Zoe gave each other another what-is-he-talking-about look. They'd already tested the theory that the necklace was stolen with a robotic arm. It wasn't possible. The space under the door was too narrow, and even if it was wider, there wasn't a straight path from the door to the pedestal.

"That robotics stuff?" Flora asked. "I thought it was boring."

"What do you mean?" Taylor said. "You were really good at it. Everyone was asking you for help. I thought you liked it."

"I'm good at everything," Flora snapped, dabbing a little more paint on the pedestal. "I just didn't think it was that interesting."

"I'm only saying it one more time — out. O-U-T," Nathan barked.

"Okay, but be careful," Jaden warned Nathan. "Your necklace could get stolen again."

11

"What were you talking about in there?" Zoe demanded as soon as she, Caleb, and Jaden were outside the high school. "We already proved a robotic arm couldn't have been used to take the necklace!"

"I wasn't thinking about a robotic arm that extended and retracted," Jaden explained. "I was thinking about a robotic *pedestal* that extended and retracted."

"Huh?" Caleb said, looking confused. "I don't get it."

"Me neither," Zoe admitted.

"You know how the paint on your wings cracked in the places where you folded them?" Jaden asked. Zoe nodded. "That's what gave me the idea. When I saw Flora touching up the marks on her pedestal, I started thinking that maybe the paint cracked in those circles around the base because the whole pedestal folds up the way an accordion does. Folds up and then stretches back out."

"The way the arm stretched out and back," Caleb said, starting to catch on.

"Right! I think the pedestal must have something inside it like the rubber bands and spools we used for the arm, or like the spring inside an umbrella. And I think it's something that can be worked with a remote control, the way the twins were using a remote to move the Artbot they're making," Jaden said.

"My mind is blown," Zoe said, putting her hands to her head and flinging them out with an exploding sound.

"If the pedestal was low to the ground, the thief could have shoved something really thin under the door — like a wire or a coat hanger or something — and pulled the necklace off," Jaden continued. "The necklace was thin enough to slide under."

"There's only one problem," Caleb said. "The pedestal wasn't close enough to the door for a coat hanger or a wire to reach."

"And don't forget about the spider web. That was between the pedestal and the door," Zoe added.

"I know. I was bluffing when I said I *exactly* knew how the thief stole the necklace," Jaden admitted. "I think I know part of the how — by using a pedestal that can be raised and lowered with a remote. But I haven't figured out how they got around the problem of the pedestal being so far from the door."

"You just stood there and lied?" Caleb cried. "I totally believed you."

Jaden smiled. "I want the thief to believe I know *exactly* how he or she took the necklace. If the thief wasn't in the room when I was bragging about it, hopefully he or she will hear about what I said."

Zoe frowned. "But what good will that do?"

"I'm hoping the thief will panic and do something to try to cover up their crime," Jaden answered. "That might give us the clue we need to really solve the case once and for all."

"Let me make sure I have this straight," Caleb said. "We only maybe kind of know *how* the necklace was stolen, and we don't know for sure *who* stole it."

"Well, I have my suspicions, but that's all we know right now," Jaden agreed. "We're not doomed yet. Maybe we'll know more tomorrow."

* * *

The next day, Mrs. Ram rushed into science class a few seconds after the bell rang.

"Ooooh, Mrs. Ram's late," someone called.

Mrs. Ram didn't laugh like she normally would have. Instead, she said, "Mr. Leavey and I just realized something is missing from the makerspace in the media center." She looked over at Thing One and Thing Two. "I'm sorry, but your Artbot has been stolen."

"No —" Benjamin began.

"— way!" Samuel finished.

"When I find out who took it, they're going to be in big trouble!" Sonja exclaimed.

Jaden scribbled a note. He passed it to Zoe, who read it and passed it to Caleb. It said: "My bluff worked. The thief made a move. I'm sure he/she took the Artbot because he/she used something like it to steal the necklace."

"Mr. Leavey and I are going to make sure you two get everything you need to make a new one," Mrs. Ram told the twins. "We'll find the funds somewhere."

"Do you know —" Benjamin began.

"— who did it?" Samuel finished.

Mrs. Ram shook her head. "I'm sorry, but we don't. We found this on the ground, though." She held up a folded piece of pale-green paper. "We think whoever took the Artbot might have accidentally left this behind."

"Would it be okay for me to
look at it?" Zoe asked.

"Do you recognize it?" Mrs. Ram asked as she
handed the sheet of paper to Zoe.

Zoe unfolded it. There was a lily pad printed on the
top, and underneath was a note: "Taylor will never love
you as much as I do. It's impossible. Let me prove it to
you." No one had signed it.

"I haven't seen it before," Zoe replied. She showed it
to Jaden. "Have you?"

Jaden shook his head, then handed the note to Caleb.
Caleb shook his head too and handed the note back to
Mrs. Ram.

Mrs. Ram walked back to the front of the classroom
just as an idea shot into Zoe's brain. She snatched up
her pencil and wrote a note of her own. She passed it to
Jaden, who read it first and then passed it to Caleb. It
said:

I know who stole the necklace — Flora, the frog lover!! Of course she'd use green paper with a lily pad on it.

<u>Motive</u>: She loves Nathan!!! That's why she took the necklace. She was jealous because Nathan made it for Taylor — with aquamarines that matched Taylor's eyes. So romantic!!! Flora had a huge scowl on her face when Nathan was taking pictures of Taylor with the necklace on. So jealous!!!

Flora didn't want to hurt Nathan, though. She still wanted him to have a necklace in the show (displayed on her pedestal). She gave him the pearls, because pearls are her favorites. She was probably hoping he'd give the new necklace to her — once she got up the guts to give him the note that said she looooved him.

Zac said Flora was good at robotics, and Kylie said Flora was really smart. Flora could have totally figured out how to make the pedestal fold up and move around using a remote.

Case closed!!!!!

12

That afternoon after school, Caleb, Zoe, and Jaden were huddled together near the gallery room. People were wandering in and out, looking at the exhibits. Mrs. Ram and Mr. Leavey had just gone in. The librarian's shirt had been buttoned wrong.

"I say we just go to Mrs. Ram and tell her Flora is the necklace thief," Caleb said. "We know how she stole it, and why she stole it, and everything."

"We know, but we don't have evidence," Jaden answered.

"We need proof," Zoe agreed.

"The twins used a cell to control their bot. Maybe Flora used a cell as a remote too," Caleb said. "If we could get her phone —"

Zoe didn't let him finish. "On it!" She hurried into the gallery room and pinched the bridge of her nose really hard — hard enough that she got tears in her eyes — then she rushed over to Flora. "Can I borrow your cell?" she asked, trying to make her voice quaver a little. "I'm worried about my sister. Kylie was supposed to meet me here, and she's never late. I think something bad might have happened. My parents won't let me have a cell. They say I'm too young."

"Um, okay." Flora pulled her cell out of her pocket and handed it over. Zoe went straight out into the hall and handed it to Jaden.

He flipped it open one-handed, did some scrolling, then said, "Show time!"

Mrs. Ram and Mr. Leavey were just leaving the room as the three of them started in.

"Can you stay a few more minutes?" Jaden asked. "There's something you should see."

"Sure," Mrs. Ram said. "What is it?"

"I think it's better if you see for yourself," Zoe answered.

Jaden walked around the spider-web display and over to Flora's pedestal. The others followed.

Nathan and Flora were both standing there. "I told you to stop coming over here," Nathan said.

Jaden didn't answer. Instead he pressed a button on the cell. There was a crackling sound as the pedestal collapsed into itself. The sound of paint cracking.

Mrs. Ram gasped.

"No way," Nathan breathed.

"Give me back my phone!" Flora cried.

"I'm almost done with it," Jaden told her. He pressed another button on the cell, and the pedestal began to move. It maneuvered around the spider-web display and stopped when it got to the gallery door. "Caleb, you want to show them the rest?"

"Mr. Leavey, do you have a piece of wire?" Caleb asked. Mr. Leavey's pockets were almost as good as a makerspace.

The librarian fumbled in his pocket and handed Caleb a folded piece of wire. Caleb took it, straightened it out, made a hook in one end, then ran out of the room. He slammed the door behind him.

"Pretend that door is locked," Zoe said loudly enough for everyone in the room to hear. A second later, the wire poked under the door. The hooked end slid over the top of the pedestal. It left a few scratches before it snagged the necklace, pulling it off the top of the pedestal and under the door.

"Pretend I'm outside that door you're pretending is locked," Jaden said. He pushed a few buttons on the cell phone, and the pedestal rose back to its original height. As it glided over to the other side of the spider-web display, Zoe noticed the pedestal now had white circles around the base in several places where the paint had cracked.

Caleb burst back into the room. "I'm not going to jail!" he yelled. Jaden and Zoe clapped. Everyone else looked confused.

Jaden held the cell phone out to Flora. "Here's your remote control back," he said. "I mean your cell phone."

"You did it?" Nathan cried. "You stole my necklace?"

Flora snatched the phone from Jaden and ran out of the room. Nathan stared after her. "I'm sorry," he finally said, looking from Zoe to Caleb. "I really thought one of you did it. I can't believe it was Flora. I've known her forever. We were in preschool together."

"She did it because she likes you," Zoe explained. "She was jealous that you made the necklace for Taylor."

"I'm going to find Taylor and tell her what happened," Nathan said. "Then I guess we'll try to find Flora. She and Taylor have been friends a long time too." He started out the door, then turned back. "Sorry again."

"It's okay," Caleb answered, and Zoe nodded.

"She's the one who took the twins' Artbot too," Jaden told Mrs. Ram and Mr. Leavey. "She used the same kind of giant Roomba-ish thing for the bottom of the pedestal. Yesterday I said I knew how the necklace had been stolen because we'd been using leftovers from the exhibit in the science club. I said it in front of Flora."

"She must have panicked and decided to grab the Artbot. I don't know how she thought it would help her," Mrs. Ram said.

"I think she thought that if we didn't have it, we wouldn't be able to prove it. But all it did was help us figure out how she got the pedestal near the door," Jaden said.

Mr. Leavey gently tilted the pedestal up and peered underneath. "Yeah, it's exactly the same kind of disk with treads that the twins used."

"We think there's got to be something like the bands and spools we used to make the JadArm stretch out inside the pedestal," Zoe told Mrs. Ram and Mr. Leavey. "Or even something like the inside of an umbrella."

"I'm impressed. I don't know how you three pieced all this together," Mrs. Ram said.

"Turns out that you haven't just been teaching us to be scientists," Caleb told her.

Jaden smiled at Mrs. Ram. "You've also been teaching us how to be detectives. Everything we've been working on in the club helped us crack the case."

Zoe gave a little hop. "The Case of the Invisible Robot!"

About the Author

Melinda Metz is the author of more than sixty books for teens and kids, including *Echoes* and the young adult series Roswell High, the basis of the TV show *Roswell*. Her middle-grade mystery *Wright and Wong: Case of the Nana-Napper* (co-authored by the fabulous Laura J. Burns) was a juvenile Edgar finalist. Melinda lives in Concord, North Carolina, with her dog, Scully, a pen-eater just like the dog who came before her.

About the Illustrator

Heath McKenzie is a best-selling author and illustrator from Melbourne, Australia. Over the course of his career, he has illustrated numerous books, magazines, newspapers, and even live television. As a child, Heath was often inventing things, although his inventions didn't always work out as planned. His inventions still only work some of the time . . . but that's the fun of experimenting!

Glossary

accuse (uh-KYOOZ) — to say a person has done something wrong or illegal

evidence (EV-uh-duhnss) — information and facts that help prove something is true

gallery (GAL-uh-ree) — a place where works of art are hung or put out for people to look at

logically (LOJ-ik-lee) — using careful and correct reason and thinking

makeshift (MEYK-shift) — having been put together quickly with what was available and only meant to be used for a short period of time

maneuver (muh-NOO-ver) — to move carefully

motive (MOH-tiv) — the reason someone did something

pendulum (PEN-juh-luhm) — an object made of a stick or string with a weight attached at the bottom so that it swings back and forth freely

physics (FIZ-iks) — the science that deals with matter and energy, including the study of light, heat, sound, electricity, motion, and force

precision (pri-SIZH-uhn) — extreme accuracy

retract (ri-TRAKT) — to fold back into itself or oneself

suspect (SUHS-pekt) — a person who might have done something wrong and is being investigated

Discussion Questions

1. Talk about what you think happens after the story ends. What does Flora do with the necklace? Do Taylor and Nathan forgive her?

2. The high school students' exhibition, The Art of Science, shows how art and science are connected. However, sometimes people think art and science are complete opposites and that one is more important than the other. How do you feel? Talk about your opinion.

3. As you were reading, who did you think was going to be guilty of stealing the necklace? Discuss why and try to use examples from the book.

Writing Prompts

1. Robots and machines are often designed to make it easier, faster, or safer to do a certain task. Jaden, Caleb, and Zoe's invention, the JadArm, will help Jaden reach things more easily. Think about an invention that could help you, and write a paragraph about what it does and how it works.

2. The S.MA.R.T.S. friends had a lot of suspects in this case. Write a list of the suspects and the reasons why each of them might have stolen the necklace.

3. We use many different types of technology each and every day. Write a paragraph about a piece of technology you love using and why. Then write another paragraph about a piece of technology you don't like using and why.

Makerspaces and Robotics Clubs

There are plenty of groups like S.M.A.R.T.S. that are perfect for curious kids interested in technology. Makerspaces and robotics clubs are just some of the hands-on ways you can explore your interest in science and engineering and really get creative.

A makerspace is a community space that provides tools and materials for kids to work on individual projects. Makerspaces can look very different from place to place. Some spaces may have hi-tech tools like 3-D printers, while others might have cardboard and hot glue guns. They sometimes focus on specific types of subjects — like robotics, electronics, computer coding, sewing and textiles, or woodworking. But no matter what the makerspace has or focuses on, the goal is always the same: to learn and discover by doing hands-on projects that are only limited by your imagination. And once you're done building whatever you thought up, you could show it off at a Maker Faire. The Maker Faire is an event where people of all ages who love to build and tinker can showcase their creations.

Robotics clubs are all about designing, building, and programming robots. Clubs often have more specific activities and might teach teamwork by having students work together on one robot. A robotics club might even participate in one of the many regional or national robotics competitions, like BEST (Boosting Engineering, Science, and Technology) or FIRST (For Inspiration and Recognition of Science and Technology), where teams are challenged to build a robot that can perform a specific task.

More adventure and science mysteries!

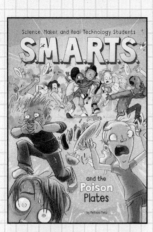

www.capstonepub.com